NICK JR.

DORA the EXPLORER® It's Sharing Day!

by Kirsten Larsen   illustrated by Ron Zalme

SIMON AND SCHUSTER/NICKELODEN

Based on the TV series *Dora the Explorer* as seen on Nick Jr.

SIMON AND SCHUSTER
First published in Great Britain in 2007 by Simon & Schuster UK Ltd
Africa House, 64-78 Kingsway, London WC2B 6AH
A CBS COMPANY

Originally published in the USA in 2006 by Simon Spotlight,
an imprint of Simon & Schuster Children's Division, New York.

A CIP catalogue record for this book is available from the British Library

ISBN -10: 184738014X
ISBN - 13: 9781847380142
Printed in China

¡Hola! Today is Sharing Day! Boots and I are going to *Abuela*'s house for a very special lunch. We are all bringing food to share. *Abuela* is making *empanadas*. Boots is bringing bananas. For dessert I am bringing rice and milk so we can make *arroz con leche*.

Before we go to *Abuela*'s house, we have to get the milk and rice for our dessert. Will you help us? Great!

Map says we need to go to Benny's Barn to get the milk. Then we need to go to the Rice Fields to get some rice. Let's hurry so we can get to *Abuela*'s in time for lunch. Come on! *¡Vámonos!*

Look, there's Benny in his go-cart.

Hola, Benny! Boots and I were coming to see you. We need to borrow some milk from you. Will you give us a ride to the Barn so we can borrow some milk?

Benny said he'll share his go-cart with us and give us a ride to the Barn. Hop on! *Gracias*, Benny!

We made it to Benny's Barn!
¡Mira! There's Benny's grandma. *¡Hola!* We need to borrow some milk so we can make *arroz con leche* for our Sharing Day lunch. Will you share some milk with us? You will? *¡Gracias!*

Since Benny and his grandma have shared with us, let's invite them to our Sharing Day lunch. They said they would bring some cowboy cookies to share. *¡Delicioso!*

Where do we need to go now? We have to go to the Rice Fields to get some rice. We can take a shortcut through Isa's Flowery Garden. *¡Vámonos!* Let's go!

There are so many plants and flowers in Isa's Flowery Garden. Some of the flowers are so tall that we can't see around them. How will we know which way to go?

I hear someone singing. *¿Quién está cantando?* Who is singing?

¡Sí! It's Isa!

Isa is singing a special flower song for us. She's making the flowers move and dance! Now we can pass by them and follow the path! *Gracias,* Isa!

Isa shared her flower song to help us find our way through her Flowery Garden. Since Isa shared something with us, let's invite her to our Sharing Day lunch too!

Isa will bring a fresh vegetable salad to share. Yum!

Uh-oh. It's almost lunchtime, and we still need to go to the Rice Fields to get some rice for our dessert. How can we get there quickly?

Look, there's Tico in his plane. Let's ask Tico if he can help.

Tico is going to share his plane and give us a ride to the Rice Fields. *Gracias*, Tico. *¡Vámonos!*

We made it to the Rice Fields. To get the rice, we have to shake the rice plants. Will you count the rice plants you see? *¡Uno, dos, tres, cuatro, cinco!* Five rice plants!

Good job! Now we have enough rice to make *arroz con leche* for everyone.

Now let's go to *Abuela*'s house for lunch. Since Tico shared his plane with us, let's invite him to come along. He's bringing yummy nut bread to share. *¡Muy bien!*

Yay! We made it to *Abuela*'s house. Now *Abuela* has the milk and rice for our *arroz con leche*. She is making it right now. Mmm. It smells yummy. I can't wait to eat!

Lunchtime! Look at all of this delicious food we can share. We have *empanadas*, bananas, cowboy cookies, vegetable salad, nut bread, and *arroz con leche* for dessert!

¡Vamos a comer! Let's go eat!

What a great Sharing Day! Benny shared his go-cart,
Isa shared her song, Tico shared his plane, and everyone
brought food to share for lunch.

What did you share today?